SNOW WHITE
AND THE
SEVEN DWARFS
EASY TO READ AND COLOR

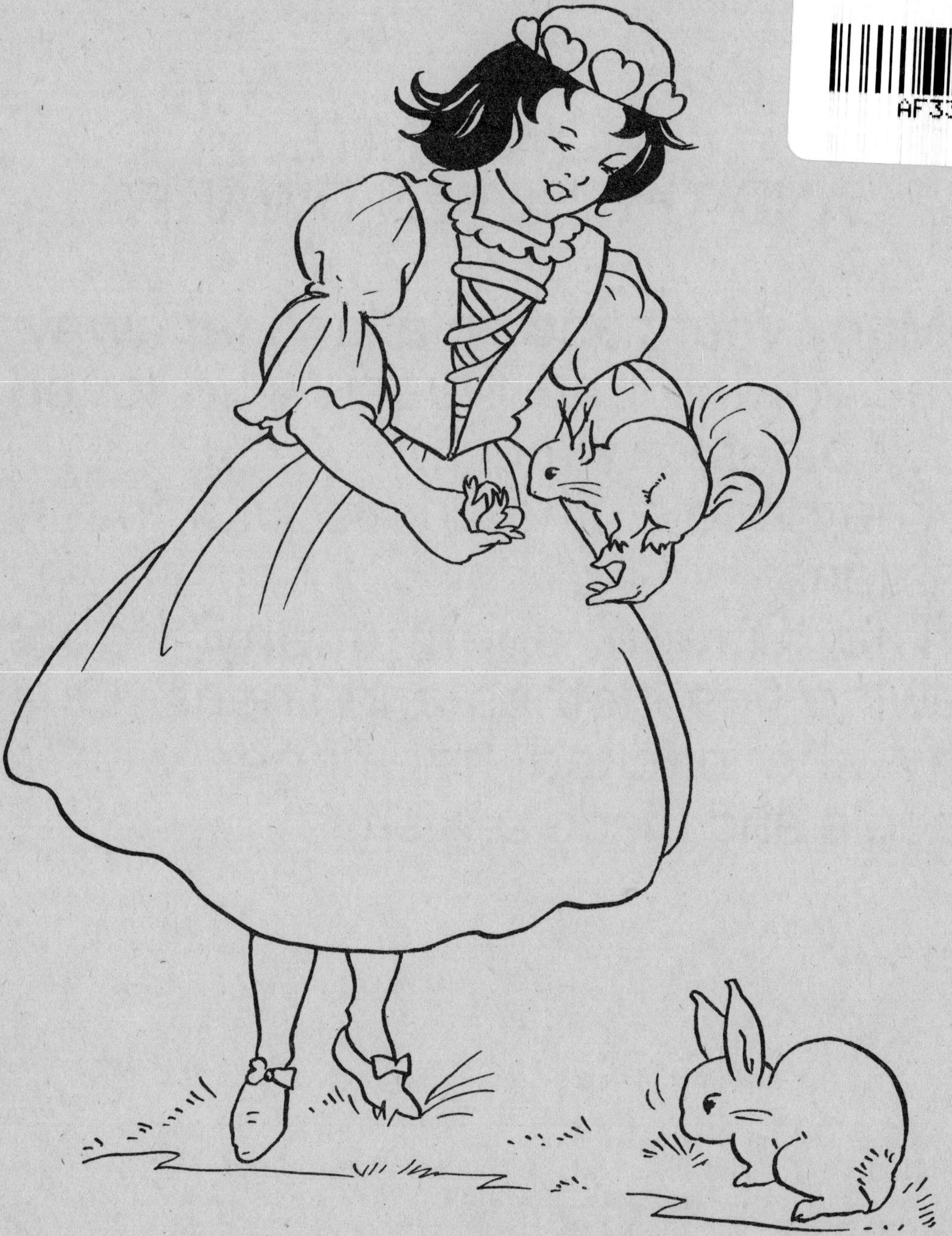

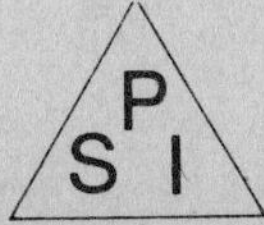

P.S.I. & Associates, inc.
10481 S.W. 123rd Street
Miami, Florida 33176

SNOW WHITE
AND THE SEVEN DWARFS

Many years ago, in a land far away, lived a King and Queen who loved each other very much.

They had a fine castle with lovely gardens.

The Queen spent many hours sewing fine clothes and linens. One day she pricked her finger with a needle and made a wish.

"If only we had a child," she thought, "my happiness would be complete."

In time, the Queen had a baby girl. She was born on a clear day, with snow on the ground.

The little girl was named Snow White.

She was a happy baby, laughing and playing in her cradle.

Her parents thought she was the most wonderful child in the world.

Before long, the Queen died. A few years later, the King married again.

The new Queen was very beautiful. She was also very vain and very wicked.

Every day she looked into her Magic Mirror, asking, "Mirror, mirror on the wall, who is the fairest one of all?"

The mirror always answered, "You O Queen, are the fairest one of all." This pleased the Queen.

As Snow White grew older, she became a beautiful young Princess. She was loved by everyone in the kingdom.

Soon the King, too, died. The wicked Queen was left to care for Snow White. She was jealous of the little girl.

One day when she asked, "Mirror, mirror on the wall, who is the fairest one of all?" the answer made her very angry.

This time the mirror answered, "Snow White is the fairest one of all."

The Queen was furious! She thought of a plan to get rid of Snow White.

She sent for one of the King's hunters. She ordered him to take the little Princess into the forest and kill her.

She never wanted to see Snow White again.

The hunter was kind and very fond of Snow White. He decided not to carry out the Queen's command.

Instead, he thought of a way to save the little girl's life.

Snow White was happy to be walking though the forest. She skipped along, enjoying the trees and flowers.

She listened to the birds singing, and to the small animal noises around her.

When they were deep into the forest, the hunter told Snow White that he had to leave her.

"You must never come back to the palace," he said.

"The Queen is very jealous. She wants to be rid of you. Surely you will find a kind woodcutter in the forest who will let you stay with his family. Then you will be happy."

At first, Snow White was frightened.
Soon she saw that the animals were very friendly. Squirrels and rabbits came to play near her.

After a while, it started to get dark.

Snow White knew that she had to find a place to sleep. She saw a path and followed it through the trees.

The path led her to a small house in a clearing.

"Maybe the people who live here will let me stay with them," she thought.

It looked like such a friendly little house with its thatched roof and diamond-shaped windows.

There were flowers in the garden. Snow White walked to the door and knocked.

No one seemed to be at home. Snow White opened the door and walked in.

There she saw a table and seven small chairs. On the table were seven bowls.

"Seven very small people must live here," thought Snow White. "I hope they will be kind and let me stay with them."

Snow White wanted to be helpful. She washed the dishes and swept the floors.

Then she prepared dinner with food she found in the kitchen. It smelled delicious.

Upstairs she found a room with seven small beds.

Suddenly, she felt very tired. She curled up on one of the beds and fell asleep.

The small house belonged to seven dwarfs. They spent their days digging for gold and jewels in the mountains nearby.

Early every morning, they left the house with shovels. Each evening, they returned with sacks filled with treasure.

They always sang as they walked home through the forest.

The dwarfs were pleasant-looking little men.

They all had white beards and wore different shaped hats.

They carried lanterns to light their way. And they had their shovels and sacks with them.

They were singing and smiling, as usual, as they hurried home after a full day's work.

When the dwarfs arrived home, they knew someone had been in their house. It smelled so good and looked so clean.

They wondered who had been there. They decided to look around.

"Bring a lantern," one of the little men said. "We will look upstairs. Maybe the stranger is still here."

Quietly, they went up the stairs.

They walked into the bedroom.

Sure enough, there was Snow White still sound asleep.

"How beautiful she is," said one.

"Shall we wake her and find out who she is?" whispered another.

The voices awakened Snow White. She sat up, amazed to see the seven little men standing around the bed.

Snow White told them how she found their house in the forest. And she told them about her wicked stepmother.

"The new Queen wants to be rid of me forever," she said.

The dwarfs felt sorry for the princess. They said she could stay with them as long as she liked.

"Thank you! Thank you!" she said. And she hugged each one.

That night the jealous Queen asked the mirror who was the fairest one of all. She could hardly believe the answer,

"In the forest, with seven
dwarfs small
Lives Snow White, the fairest
of all."

The Queen was really angry. She dressed herself as an old woman. Carrying a basket, she walked to the dwarfs' cottage in the forest.

"Come see what I have," the old woman called to Snow White. "This pretty ribbon will look beautiful on your dress. Here, let me lace it up for you."

Snow White liked the bright ribbon. She let the old woman tie it around her.

It was tied so tight that Snow White could hardly breathe. She fell to the floor immediately.

Luckily, the dwarfs came home in time to save her.

Snow White was very happy living in the little cottage. She kept the house clean and neat.

She cooked delicious meals for the dwarfs. They enjoyed eating whatever she prepared.

Snow White was never lonely. The small forest animals were friendly and came to visit her. She was always busy while the dwarfs were working.

One day the mirror again told the Queen that Snow White was the fairest. The Queen was angrier than ever.

"This time," she thought, "I will get rid of her for good!"

She dressed herself as a pleasant-looking lady and went back to the cottage with a basket of combs. She showed them to Snow White.

"See how beautiful these are," she said.

The lady looked kind. The combs were lovely.

Snow White let the lady put a comb into her shining black hair.

But the comb was sharp and had poison on its ends.

Immediately, Snow White fell to the ground.

Again, the dwarfs came home in time to save her.

The dwarfs were worried about Snow White.

"Never open the door for anybody," said one.

"Do not talk to strangers," said another.

"You must keep the door locked," said the third.

The others added, "And the windows." "The wicked Queen may come back." "She is trying to kill you." "Stay in the house and you will be safe."

Snow White promised to be careful. Every day, when the dwarfs left, she locked herself in the cottage.

She was busy every day. She cooked and cleaned and sewed.

Her animal friends came to visit.

And the mirror still told the Queen that Snow White was the fairest one of all.

"Snow White cannot be saved this time," said the Queen to herself. "This will be the end of her!"

She dressed herself as a happy, kind farmer's wife.

Then she took a rosy red apple and poisoned one side.

When she got to the cottage and knocked, Snow White did not open the door.

"Come to the window, then," said the woman. "I am taking these fine apples to the market. Would you like one?"

"It is quite safe and delicious," laughed the woman. "See, I will bite this side. You can taste the other side."

The old woman took a bite and smiled.

Snow White opened the window and reached for the apple.

Snow White took a bite from the other side of the apple.

At once, she fell down dead.

The Queen was delighted. She hurried back to the castle.

When the dwarfs came home, they found Snow White and the poisoned apple. They tried to wake her. They rubbed her hands and put water on her forehead.

Nothing they did awakened Snow White.

The dwarfs were very, very sad. The next day they built a beautiful glass box for her. They placed Snow White inside with many flowers around her.

The rabbits and squirrels and birds were sad. They came to watch over Snow White.

The little men went to work each day, but they were too sad to sing on their way home.

One day, a handsome Prince came riding through the forest. He stopped when he saw the beautiful girl.

The dwarfs were at home and told the Prince about Snow White and the wicked Queen.

The Prince fell in love with Snow White. He opened the glass case and kissed her. She opened her eyes, and stepped out.

"Look! Look! A miracle!" the dwarfs shouted. Her animal friends danced for joy. The birds sang happily.

Snow White and the Prince knew at once that they loved each other.

"You shall come to live in my palace and marry me," the Prince said. "With me, you will be safe from the wicked Queen forever."

The dwarfs were very happy for Snow White. But they would miss her. She promised that they could come to the palace to visit her often. She and Prince would visit them, too.

Soon the Prince and Princess were married.

The dwarfs brought fine gifts from the treasures they had dug in the mountains.

Once again, the wicked Queen asked the mirror who was the most beautiful. The mirror answered,
"Snow White, married to the
Prince so tall,
Is still the fairest one
of all."
The Queen was so angry, she snatched the mirror from the wall. It broke into a million pieces.
A sharp piece of glass pierced her heart and she died at once.
Snow White and the Prince lived happily ever after.